SPELLS-A-POPPING GRANNY'S SHOPPING

Tracey
Corderoy

illustrated by

Joe Berger

nosy crow

My granny's rather . . . different,

as you can plainly see.

Her handbag pops and hisses

and her pets are . . . slippery!

Her house is in a quiet street
although it's kind of batty!

She'd have the neighbours round for tea,
except they're not that chatty.

One day, I helped my granny out.
She had so much to do.
We tidied up the kitchen shelves
and cleaned the fridge out, too.
We opened up the cupboard door...

. . . but there was NOTHING there.

"Who's eaten all the crisps?" I sighed.

"Nice pets are meant to share!"

BISCUIT

TINGLES

The bats all blushed.

The cats just shrugged.

The frogs were windy-popping.

"Don't worry, dear," my granny grinned.

"We can just go SHOPPING!"

So Granny took me to the shops.
"No crazy stuff," I said.

But Granny didn't seem to hear
and waved her wand instead.
"Oh, no!" I gulped. My eyes grew wide
as magic filled the air . . .

. . . and biscuits danced
and popcorn popped . . . .

. . . and soap chased underwear!

Next, Granny found the runner beans
and sent them on a race.
"Get ready. . .
steady. . .
RUN!" she cried.
I groaned and
hid my face.

Now Granny magicked animals off boxes, jars and tins.
Small yappy dogs and guinea pigs
and cats with Cheshire grins.

Fish fingers sprouted heads and tails
and swam off to the door,
whilst leaving itty-bitty trails
of breadcrumbs on the floor!

"Oh, Granny,
what a mess!" I cried.
She'd gone too far again.
I shook my head and Granny blushed,
"I'll clean it up." But then . . .

. . . I spied a really naughty thing,
a truly dreadful sight —
two robbers filling up their sack.
"Oh, no!"
I gasped in fright.

I showed my granny. "Pah!" she said.
"We'll get that rotten pair!
Now, let me think . . .
what can we use?
Ah, yes —
this chocolate bear!"

My granny grinned and swished her wand,
and with a giant –

pop!

– the chocolate bear
sprang into life . . .

. . . and made those robbers stop!

Some officers appeared and took the horrid thieves away.
Then everybody clapped and cheered and shouted,
"Hip hooray!"

"Oh, Granny, you're the best!" I said.
"So what if you are wild!"

"You are you
and I am me,
and we're a team!"
I smiled.

At home, my granny cooked us up
a tasty treat for two.

"Just as you like it,
dear!" she winked.

"No flies
or froggy-poo!"

Then suddenly
the doorbell rang.

DING DONG!

Who could it be . . . ?

Just look who's here!
It's party-time.